David's Valuable Lesson

Insight from an Unlikely Source

Written by

Santosh Ninan

Illustrated by

Marie Sanderson

To Elvera
Love Auntie
Emerald

Merry Christmas
'20

Halo
PUBLISHING
INTERNATIONAL

ISBN: 978-1-61244-918-0
LCCN: 2020919339

Halo Publishing International, LLC
8000 W Interstate 10, Suite 600
San Antonio, Texas 78230
www.halopublishing.com

Printed and bound in the United States

This book is dedicated to my parents,
Abraham and Leela Ninan.
You taught me the most important lessons.

I love you.

A long time ago, there lived a donkey named David.

He was smaller than the other donkeys. He was also sort of clumsy.

4

When the young donkeys played *Step over the Logs*, he tripped. And it was even worse when they played *Tip the Bucket*.

Sometimes, the other donkeys laughed and made fun of David.

They stood close together, blocking him from the trough at feeding time.

Many days David walked
through the fields alone.

When night fell, David lay on the straw and looked up at the dark, star-filled sky.

He thought to himself:

What good am I?

I'm not fast or strong like all the other donkeys.

What can I do?

I wish I were special.

8

This was David's wish – to feel special,
to feel like he mattered and was important.

He never told anyone his secret wish.

Some nights he felt so sad that he would cry quietly.

One day, David found himself alone in his stable.

A man came into the stable.

He looked around and fixed his eyes on David.

He walked over to David, looked him over and said to David's owner, "This is the one. My master needs this one."

David's owner tried to talk the man into taking another donkey.

"No one has ridden this donkey. He's small and clumsy."

But the other man insisted.

David was puzzled.

Where was he going? Who was this man? What was happening?

The man led David through the winding streets of the city.

And then they stopped.

Another man walked up to David.

This man had kind eyes. He looked at David and gently patted him.

And just like that
– the man with kind eyes
was sitting on David!

Wow!

David had NEVER given anyone a ride before!

David walked slowly and carefully.

He didn't want to stumble in the crowded streets.

The man guided David on the path he should take.

As they traveled, David looked around and noticed something.

There were a lot more people crowding close to the man.

They had palm branches in their hands.

They waved the branches and shouted!

David perked his ears up.

"Hosanna!

Blessed is he who comes in the name of the Lord!

Hosanna in the highest heaven!

Hosanna!"

A big donkey grin spread across David's face.

This was the greatest moment in his life!

People continued to cheer as he trotted
along with his head held high.

This is it!

People are seeing the real me!

I am the greatest donkey of all time!

I AM SPECIAL!

But all of a sudden, everything ended!

The man with the kind eyes hopped
off David, gave him a pat on the
head and was on his way.

No more crowds.

No more cheering.

David was led to another stable.

And it became very quiet, the kind of quiet when you can hear your thoughts clearly.

David lay down in the straw.

David was confused, angry and sad, all at the same time.

What just happened?

Where did everybody go?

Now, what do I do?

As David lay there, thinking, another donkey walked over to him.

"Hi," said the other donkey.

David noticed it was an older donkey.

"Hi," David answered softly.

"You look sad. What's wrong?"

"Well, you see, I was carrying a man into town. And I was doing such a great job that a big crowd gathered around me and were cheering and waving palm branches! I was so excited! And then — it all stopped. And here I am, all alone again, just like before."

17

The older donkey gave a little donkey laugh,
which sounded a lot like "HEE HAW!"

David got angry. "Hey! What's so funny? It isn't funny!"

"I'm sorry," the older donkey said. "You don't
know who your rider was, do you?"

"No."

"That man was Jesus. The people weren't cheering you.
They were cheering Jesus!"

David looked up, "They were? Who is Jesus?"

"Who is Jesus? Why Jesus is the most wonderful person ever! Jesus is kind and loving.

He can heal sick people, and I even heard he raised people from the dead!

That's why people were cheering for him!"

"Oh." David looked down at the ground, feeling very silly. "Makes sense. Why would anyone cheer for me—a dumb, clumsy donkey?"

"Hey, hang on! Don't talk like that! You're not dumb or clumsy! Can't you see? Jesus could have picked any donkey in the world, but he chose you. Think about it! You carried Jesus!"

"So?"

"So! If you hadn't carried him, the people couldn't have seen him. And if they couldn't have seen him, they couldn't have praised him!" The older donkey stamped his foot.

"You see, we can have all kinds of jobs in this life. But, the only job that really matters is the job YOU did! You showed all of us—our real job is to lift Jesus higher than ourselves so that other people can see him. They don't need to see us or what we do. It's only important that they see him."

"How do you know all this stuff? You're just a donkey like me," David said.

"You're
right. Let me
tell you. I once had
to carry somebody important
too. There once was a young woman
who was going to have a baby. She was quite
nervous about it. I had to carry her with her husband
leading us—for a long, long time.

We finally got to a stable that I thought was going
to be for me. But it was actually for the baby. She had
her baby there—in the stable!

And the baby, you're not going to believe this. That baby
grew up to be Jesus!

I mean—he WAS Jesus!"

David tried to take all this in. He wandered over to a corner of the stable.

I carried Jesus. Jesus could have chosen any donkey, but he chose me.

And this was David's valuable lesson. David learned that despite being small and sometimes clumsy— he now knew deep in his heart where no one can touch, that he was special.

And what is true for David is true for all of us. Each one of us has a special job to do. We can all lift Jesus higher than us. And when we do that, we discover, just like David, that we are important too!